The
MAGIC
UNICORN

For Colin — M.M.

For Claire and Nick
with love — C.R.

First North American edition 1996
Published by
Marlowe & Company,
632 Broadway, Seventh Floor,
New York, NY 10012

Edited by A.J. Wood
Designed by Janie Louise Hunt

ISBN 1-56924-785-4

Printed and bound in Belgium

The MAGIC UNICORN

Written by Caroline Repchuk
Illustrated by Moira Maclean

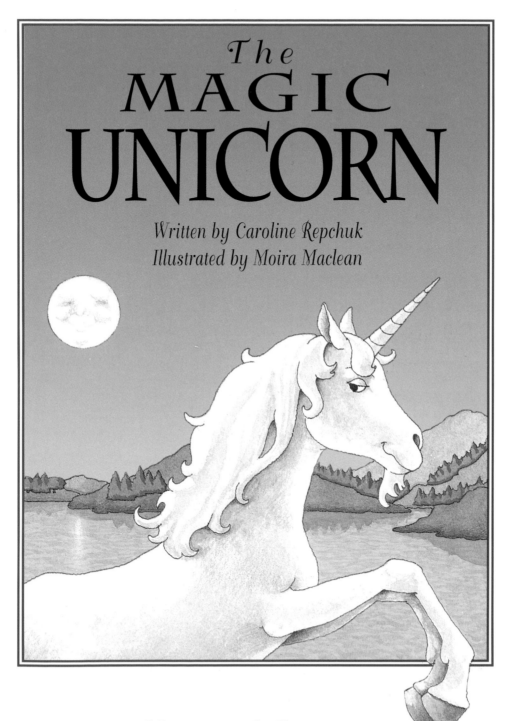

MARLOWE & COMPANY
NEW YORK

DEEP IN THE HEART of the Emerald Forest lived a unicorn called Sebastian. Not any old common or garden unicorn, mind you, but the most beautiful unicorn in the world. Sebastian sparkled and shimmered, he razzled and dazzled, and people came from miles around just to catch a glimpse of his magical beauty.

He didn't have many fans amongst the forest folk, though. They thought he was far too full of his own importance, and it was time someone taught him a lesson!

Now, in the middle of the Emerald Forest there was a pool. It was the home of Trevor, a horribly warty old toad — just the kind any self-respecting witch loves to use in her spells. And it so happened that that morning, in the Whispering Woods on the far side of the pool, a fiendishly wicked witch put her cauldron on to boil, and then realised she was clean out of fresh toads to put in it! Now she was hot on Trevor's heels and it would be frog's legs for him if he couldn't find someone to help. So he went to see Sebastian.

Luckily, Sebastian was bored, so he listened to Trevor's plight. He heard how the Wicked Witch had poisoned the forest pool so that Trevor could not hide there.

"Oh, please, your Worship," begged Trevor. "A quick dip of your magic horn is all it will take to make the pool safe again!"

"And why, may I ask," said Sebastian, looking down his elegant white nose in disdain, "should I help a repulsive creature like you?"

"Well, you never know, your Lordship,"
said Trevor, "one day I might be able
to do a good turn for you!"
"Hmm, hardly likely," said Sebastian,
"but since I am *so* kind and generous,
I'll help you out just this once."
With a dip of Sebastian's magical
shimmering horn the water cleared,
and with a mighty leap, Trevor
dove deep and was gone.

Finding himself beside the forest pool, Sebastian decided it was a fine opportunity to put an hour or two to good use by looking at himself. Sebastian often spent hours marvelling at his glorious reflection in the forest pool. In fact, he once gazed for so long that he fell asleep on his feet, and woke up with a loud SPLASH! when he fell in! That played havoc with his shampoo and set! It took weeks to get the pondweed out!

Sebastian was so busy admiring himself that he didn't notice the arrival of the Wicked Witch. She had had her eye on him for a while. His magic powers were legendary, and she planned to use them to make herself beautiful too. All she had to do was catch him...

Creeping up behind him, she pulled a large pair of scissors from her cape! One swift snip, and a piece of Sebastian's sparkling mane was hers!

Sebastian was furious! With a terrifying snort, he turned on his heels and chased the Wicked Witch deep into the Whispering Woods!

Little did Sebastian know that the crafty witch had a cunning plan! She darted through the dark and dangerous woods as fast as her knobbly knees would carry her, with Sebastian in hot pursuit. Reaching the middle of the woods, she darted behind a huge tree, and the unicorn went careering CRASH! into it! With a groan he realised that his precious horn was stuck fast. "I can't believe I fell for that old trick," he muttered.

In a flash the Wicked Witch locked Sebastian inside a cage, and threw the key deep into the forest pool.

"Aha! Now you are mine!" she cackled. "Let's see what magic you can do! Start by making my hair sparkle and shine like yours!"

"And what if I don't feel like it?" sneered Sebastian.

"Then I'll turn you into a toad!" said the witch. Sebastian thought of the repulsively warty Trevor and shuddered. He decided to do as he was told. So he shut his eyes and muttered a magic spell. But now that he was locked up, his magic powers were fading fast. He opened his eyes to find that, instead of having sparkling locks, the witch was completely bald!

If you've never seen a witch when she's cross, then you're lucky. It's not a pretty sight! Sebastian tried to make amends for making her bald, but he was so unhappy that his magic sparkle disappeared completely and all his spells went wrong.

The Wicked Witch wasn't happy when he made her nose grow to her knees. And she wasn't happy when he made her as fat as a pumpkin. In fact, she was so angry that she told him he had one day left to make her as beautiful as a princess, or it was pond life for him!

That night Sebastian cried big, salty tears, as he sat alone in his cage.

"I'll never escape now my magic power has gone," he sobbed. "No one will even care if I get turned into a toad!"

"I will," said a gruff voice from below. "I don't want you messing about in my pond!" It was Trevor. "I've brought some friends with me. We'll soon get you out, but first you must make me a promise..."

While Sebastian listened carefully, the water nymphs polished his horn and sprinkled his mane with fairy dust till his magic sparkle returned, brighter and more beautiful than ever.

Trevor explained that he had found the key to the cage in the forest pool. The water nymphs, who had been watching, told him what had happened, and he had come to repay Sebastian for helping him. "On one condition," finished Trevor. "That you lose that fancy air of yours, and start treating the forest folk kindly. There are plenty that need help, if only you'd listen. You might even make a few friends."

"Perhaps you're right," said Sebastian. "It's lonely and boring being beautiful and mysterious all the time. I suppose I could try and change."

Just then, as the water nymphs finished polishing, there was a hiss behind them. Kipper, the witch's cat, had returned from his nightly stroll and, mindful of the fact he'd be rewarded with a midnight snack, he let out a strangled wail.

"Quick!" cried Sebastian, in alarm. "He'll wake the Wicked Witch!"

•

In no time Trevor had the cage unlocked and Sebastian was free. "Hurry, all of you, jump on my back," he said. As a light went on inside the witch's cottage, Sebastian rose magically, high into the sky, and headed home toward the Emerald Forest, his flowing mane sparkling in the moonlight.

The Wicked Witch was not
giving up that easily though.
Oh, no. "Come back here, you
wretched unicorn!" she cried.
"What about my nose job?!"
With her nose still dangling to
her knees, she leapt on her
broomstick, which creaked under
her weight, and with Kipper clinging
on bravely behind she followed
Sebastian into the night!

Back in the Emerald Forest, Sebastian turned to thank Trevor.
"Is there anything I can do for you?" he asked politely.
"No thanks," said Trevor. "All that 'toad into a handsome prince' stuff never appealed to me. I'm happy just being a toad." But as they spoke, some of Sebastian's sparkle fell onto Trevor, and in a blinding flash he turned into a magnificent golden toad!

But before he had time to say thank you, the Wicked Witch appeared in the sky above them. "Not her again," groaned Trevor. "I'd turn her into a lily pad if I could. That would keep her out of trouble." With that, there was a loud bang, and the Wicked Witch mysteriously disappeared in a puff of smoke.

The very next day, a huge lily pad appeared on the pool. Trevor couldn't quite place it, but he thought there was something rather familiar about it...

These days, if you pass through the Emerald Forest, you just might find Trevor sitting on that lily pad, enjoying the peace and quiet.

And if Sebastian is nearby, don't worry. He's given up gazing at himself. He'll just be talking to his forest friends.